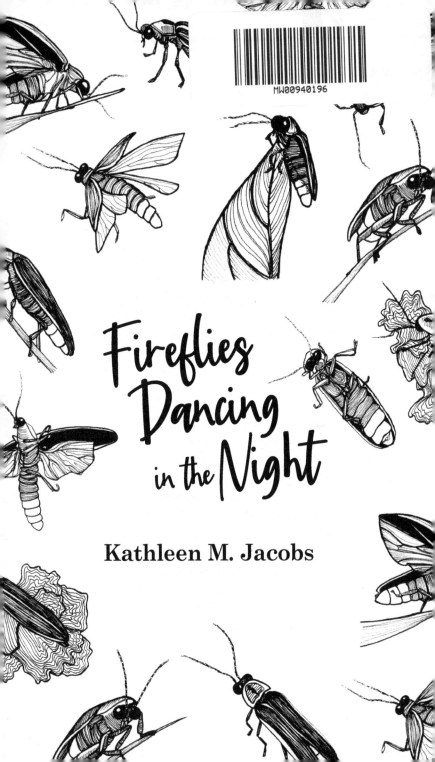

Fireflies Dancing in the Night

Kathleen M. Jacobs

Fireflies Dancing in the Night
Kathleen M. Jacobs

First Edition Published January 2021
Skippy Creek
Imprint of Jan-Carol Publishing, Inc.
Cover Art and Illustrations: Carly Thaw
Graphic Design: Tara Sizemore
Author Photo: John M. Jacobs
All rights reserved
Copyright © 2021 by Kathleen M. Jacobs

ISBN: 978-1-950895-91-5
Library of Congress Control Number: 2021931049

You may contact the publisher:
Jan-Carol Publishing, Inc.
PO Box 701
Johnson City, TN 37605
publisher@jancarolpublishing.com
jancarolpublishing.com

Jan-Carol
Publishing, Inc
"every story needs a book"

For my Godparents, Lois & George Diehl

Also by Kathleen M. Jacobs

Honeysuckle Holiday

Marble Town

Collected Curiosities: Poems, Essays, & Opinions

Please Close It!

The Puppeteer of Objects: A Lyrical Poem

Betsy Blossom Brown

Sophie & the Bookmobile

Fireflies Dancing in the Night

A Note to Young Writers:

Write your stories. Tell your stories. Sketch your stories. Write of your childhood. Write of your differences and similarities to others. Listen to the creative voices inside your heart. You will become discouraged, and that's to be expected. Do not be deterred by this interruption. Instead, choose to stay true to your vision, putting one word after another on paper, and finding joy in penning one sentence after another, until you say with complete exhilaration, "Where did that come from?!" Then you'll know that a guiding force much more powerful than yourself sprinkled a bit of fairy dust on your nearly perfect, beautiful story. And then, take a walk through nature, breathe in the freshness that is abundantly given, and move on to the next story. For there are countless others to be told and shared. THE END does not exist, for the stories we tell are as interwoven as our lives.

"No one can whistle a symphony.
It takes a whole orchestra to play it."

—H. E. Luccock, 1885–1960

Chapter One

Luna Skylar wasn't a huge fan of school except for her science and math classes, where the near-certain logic of each subject intrigued her. Her mother and father were pharmacists, and Luna always thought that she had been born with a love of numbers and measures and equations rather than letters.

She did love lower-case letters written in cursive, though—especially the letters *f* and *w*, because of their curlicues and repetition. And of course, she loved the letters *l*, *u*, *n*, and *a*, which is exactly how she wrote her name: all lower case and in cursive, whenever she could get away with it. She absolutely refused to believe the art of cursive writing was being scattered to the winds like a blown dandelion.

"Luna?" Miss Penny had called on her, but Luna was a million miles away, looking outside to the oceanic blue skies, dreaming of riding her bicycle through the late spring winds.

Luna liked every single one of the seasons, but for different, magnificent reasons, naturally. For instance, right now, she loved that spring was in full bloom. She looked out her classroom window and noticed the swaying branches of the Bradford pear trees, the delicate blooms of the weeping cherry tree, and the feather-like petals of the pink dogwood. She loved that her desk was in the row next to the window, which Miss Penny had opened just slightly so that a light, warm breeze drifted through.

Luna closed her eyes and thought of the end of school and the beginning of summer vacation. She imagined staying up later than usual, riding her bicycle up and down the hills and all along the valleys of her small town. She thought about going to the movies in the middle of the week, visiting relatives in the Midwest, and going to Myrtle Beach for two weeks with her parents and her pet hedgehog, Thistle. Suddenly, Luna felt a light touch on her arm. A pink dogwood blossom had floated through the window. When she opened her eyes, it rested on top of her desk. She didn't want to breathe for fear of it being picked up by the wind and sailing right back out the opened window.

"Luna!" Miss Penny exclaimed, startling Luna even though Miss Penny was nearly as tiny as a penny and couldn't shout, even if she tried very, very hard. Luna thought Miss Penny was beautiful, much like a ladybug, and just as graceful and colorful.

Miss Penny often wore a red paisley bandana tied in a knot at the left of her long, slender neck, which could be compared to a giraffe's— but of course nobody ever said that out loud.

She always wore what she called ballet flats, mostly of buttery black or brown leather. But

Luna's favorite pair were made of rust-colored suede and had a toe more pointed than the others, with a kiltie overlay. They all had the double-C ornamentation, embossed and outlined in heavy thread colored to match the shoe, an attached logo in a brushed silver-, gold-tone, or black enameled metal.

"My grandmother bought me my first pair of Chanel ballet flats on my sixteenth birthday and like her, I wear them every day," she would reply whenever a student asked her why she always wore ballet flats. "Must I tell you the reason yet again?" she would say, as the class giggled and begged her to talk about the lady in the black and white photograph that sat on her desk in a polished silver frame. There was a series of three tiny hearts pressed into the top of the frame, like coins in a gumball machine.

Miss Penny's skin was like poured cream. Luna liked when Miss Penny stood over her shoulder while she was at her desk and corrected something on her paper. Luna became mesmerized by the difference in their skin tones; it always made her smile, thinking about the blending of one to the other, much like a chocolate and vanilla swirl cone from the Dairy Queen. And of course, like her grandmother, Miss Penny spritzed her skin with Chanel No. 5 perfume, notes of jasmine flitting about like a gathering of finches.

Miss Penny often wore the same black or dark brown pencil skirt with a sweater set in various colors, the pearl-like buttons running from the crew neck to the bottom hem. She once told her students that she had also worn these sweater sets in college. She wore her hair the same way she had worn it in college, too: pulled back into a sleek ponytail, with a white grosgrain ribbon tied in a knot. It looked very much like a horse's mane, shiny, straight strands the color of cinnamon sprinkled on top of applesauce.

"Is it possible that Luna has spring fever?" Miss Penny said, and all the class shouted, "YES, MA'AM!" Suddenly, the mysterious trance lifted, just as the white, puffy clouds in the shape of various animals drifted past Luna's window. She giggled as well, for she had no idea how long

Miss Penny had been calling her name. Just as Luna was about to apologize for daydreaming, Miss Penny closed her book and said, with the sweetness of the dogwood blossom that Luna had pressed between the pages of her notebook, "Let's *all* have spring fever today!"

She gathered her students, held an index finger to her lips, and slipped out the back door. Once outside, they sat on a grassy knoll and looked up to the bright blue sky, studying the menagerie in the clouds. They identified first one, then another, scattering of ducks, zebras, bears, and monkeys, even a frog or two, while Miss Penny read from one of their favorite books, *A Wrinkle in Time*.

Luna looked to Miss Penny and shrugged as Miss Penny winked, smiled, and read on. Luna hoped to one day wear pencil skirts, sweater sets, and ballet flats. And she hoped, too, to treasure memories made with all her friends and relatives as much as Miss Penny outwardly treasured them.

Chapter Two

As the next month passed—much too slowly for Luna—she kept a calendar on her desk in her room, marking off each day that brought her closer and closer to the last day of school. May 26 was colored in completely with a bright pink pencil and, of course, Luna had placed a gold star sticker in the center.

Before Luna could even think of making plans for her summer vacation, she had to think of an idea for her English year-end essay. Draft after draft of proposed subjects had already been turned in to Miss Penny, who made so many suggestions for Luna to think about that it had begun to make her dizzy.

Her first idea was to write a paper about one of her heroes, Amelia Earhart, but she quickly discovered that there was simply too much information to sift through. Then she thought about interviewing her father and mother about their work as pharmacists, adding pictures of their growing collection of mortars and pestles, until she realized the information was rather lackluster; she quickly abandoned that idea. Even her parents thought it a bit dry.

"I know, why don't you write about great cyclists?" her mother suggested. Luna looked at her mother and furrowed her brow, circling her finger around her ear.

"I don't think so, Mom, but thanks anyway."

Luna's classmates had chosen subjects like "Should students be given less homework?" Luna wondered how in the world that paper could be three pages long, since the only possible answer was a resounding, "Absolutely!"

The smartest boy in Luna's class, Henry

Bloom, had chosen to write about bullying, which Luna felt would be one of the toughest topics to pick. And yet, almost everyone in Luna's class had been bullied in one way or another, and to one degree or another. Everyone, including Luna, was relieved that Henry had chosen that topic from the list they were given, because they all knew that he would do it right.

One day during a soccer game, a boy from the visiting team had called Henry "four eyes," so Henry knew first-hand all about bullies. He had been called "four eyes" before, and he had perfected a simple, three-letter word reply that always worked. It was his delivery of that word that caught every offender off-guard, and generally left them speechless. His friends had been called names too, and there were more than a few girls who liked to gossip. Because Henry was so clever and confident, and everyone wanted to be like him, his reply was, "And?" He held the soccer ball in the crook of his arm, looking over the top rim of his glasses, waiting. And when the bully had nothing to say to that simple, but very effective reply, the game continued without another incident. Genius.

Henry Bloom wanted to be a writer when he grew up, and Miss Penny agreed to let him write about bullies and those who had been bullied by making up names and certain particulars, in order to protect all his friends, neighbors, and classmates. Miss Penny was, quite simply, the best teacher ever. She always found a way to lead her students exactly where they wanted to go, long before they knew they wanted to go there. When her students arrived there, they awoke as if from a dream, wondering how in the world she did what she did. She was so clever that it didn't dawn on anyone that Miss Penny was leading them, until it did. It was like magic. And anyone who insisted on teaching the art of cursive writing was better than fine with Luna.

Just as Luna had almost settled on the idea of how to launch a school newspaper, she snapped her fingers (she really did) and thought of one of her favorite summertime adventures, knowing she had found her topic. When she announced it to Miss Penny, after having turned in one draft after another on several topics, Miss Penny thought it a grand idea. Miss Penny liked science and math best of all, even though she tried very hard not to let it show.

Chapter Three

The only thing Luna Skylar liked perhaps even more than her name was her pet hedgehog, Thistle. Then again, maybe she liked them equally as much. She also liked balance. If she could, she would like to give Thistle a playmate to keep him company when Luna was at school during the week, and her parents were at their pharmacy filling doctors' prescriptions while their customers picked up Kleenex and bath tissue, Russell Stover chocolates, and basic office supplies.

Luna had taken gymnastic classes for as

long as she could remember, and the balance beam was her favorite part of class. Every time she mounted the narrow plank of wood, she would first close her eyes and think of Mary Lou Retton, America's Sweetheart, who was also from Luna's home state, wild and wonderful West Virginia.

Luna wished she could give Thistle a pink flamingo. She could just imagine the look on Thistle's face, as he scurried hurriedly and anxiously around his sheltered space. She even imagined Thistle saying, "What in the world is *that?!*" And then Luna would show Thistle pictures of a pink flamingo balancing itself on one leg as Thistle looked on in wonderment, mimicking his new friend—whom, of course, Luna would simply name Pink. Luna knew that Thistle would understand, especially since Luna spent so much time balancing on one leg, always practicing her balance beam routine.

Eventually, Thistle would gather the courage to speak, after taking a noticeable deep breath, and say, in a language only Thistle and Pink could understand, "Well, Pink, you're absolutely stunning." Pink would reply, in a very demure tone, "Thank you, my dear. I must say, you're quite handsome," and Thistle would actually blush as he made every effort to reach his highest height, standing tall on his hind legs. And then Pink would wink.

Luna would come home from school, leaping through the front door of her house, and look at Thistle and Pink relaxing, as if they could anticipate her arrival home. In her imagination, they would be like well-behaved children, even though Luna knew they had enjoyed their time together all day long, snacking and chatting in a language all their own. Luna would know that they had taken long naps, beams of sunshine landing on them from the open windows of Luna's bedroom.

But of course, all Luna could do was tape colorful pictures of pink flamingos all over her room to keep Thistle company. She even used bright pink construction paper to cut out the letters *P-I-N-K*, taping them across the top of her favorite picture.

Luna was certain that Thistle nodded in approval with every new addition to the growing gallery of pink flamingos dancing around her room.

One day, Luna wrote an acrostic poem and tacked it to the center of her corkboard.

PLUSH PLUMAGE
INKED IN PINKS.
NESTING,
KEEN & KEMPT.

Chapter Four

O nce Luna decided on a topic for her end-of-year English essay, she found herself at her laptop, typing the word *fireflies* in the Google search box. Talk about a plethora of information! Holy cow! There were articles from so many sources that Luna struggled to pick and choose from what she thought were the most respected journals: *National Geographic* and *Scientific American*. Naturally, she started gathering her research from Wikipedia. Luna loved to say "Wikipedia;" she thought the sound of it was hilarious.

Luna found *YouTube* videos of fireflies, which she watched over and over again, a list of states where fireflies could be found, an article on what makes fireflies glow, countless papers written on which fireflies attract other fireflies and how, and the why behind the disappearance of fireflies. The last one Luna did not want to give any thought to, for the mere mention of fireflies disappearing made her very nervous; she began to chew on her fingernails, which she had been trying very hard to stop doing.

When she came across an article in *The New York Times* that talked about the mating problems of fireflies, Luna wasn't quite sure she needed to read the article, much less mention it in her essay. And yet, she didn't know why she felt that way. She did eventually read and pay close attention to an article that outlined why fireflies are facing extinction, primarily due to habitat loss, pesticides, and artificial light. After considerable thought, she chose to mention this research briefly in her essay, if for no other reason than to make Miss Penny aware of it, in case she didn't know it already.

When she came across an article in *Smithsonian*, she was delighted to learn that fireflies have their own secret language. She made a promise to herself that when they visited their relatives in the Midwest over the summer, she would listen very carefully, since the article pointed out that the light emanated from a firefly—whether male or female—is about finding a date. A date!

Luna found the article so intriguing that she sent it to her father, asking him to print a copy for her to keep. Something told Luna that she just might need it in the future, since this year she had found herself wanting to talk with Henry Bloom a bit more than she had in the past. She not only liked his name, but she liked his dark brown, curly hair that he couldn't tame. She liked that his shirt was never tucked completely inside his pants, and she liked the violet color of his eyes. Luna even liked his round, tortoise shell-framed glasses.

They reminded her a bit of John Lennon's. She wanted a pair too, but her vision was 20/20. Whenever Luna thought about Henry Bloom, she touched her forehead, finding it just a tad bit warmer than usual. And when this happened, she walked away from Henry Bloom and laughed until she was out of sight.

Chapter Five

" Fireflies!" Luna sang out from the back seat of her parents' restored 1970 steel-bodied, midnight blue Plymouth station wagon with simulated wood detailing. Luna's grandmother had driven the station wagon for as long as Luna could remember.

And like Miss Penny and her grandmother, Gram had worn Chanel No. 5 perfume since she was as young as Luna, and even spritzed her Plymouth station wagon with it. Years after Gram gave the Plymouth to Luna's dad, Luna could still smell the sweet notes of jasmine wafting through the car.

Luna ran her fingers over the brooch that had belonged to her grandmother. It was gold-toned and designed like a cluster of grapes, with tiny seed pearls. Luna wore it every day, regardless of what she chose to wear that day. It had become a part of her as much as her growing collection of Vans; her shoulder-length, springy, dark brown hair; and her forest-green, almond-shaped eyes. Around her neck, Luna always wore a silver locket with a picture of Thistle inside.

Luna's dad loved the Plymouth so much that he named it after his mother. And when Luna was born, she somehow knew before she even made an entrance that her name would be Luna, too. And all that sweetness—much like the first taste of cotton candy every summer at the fairgrounds—made Luna happy. Sometimes, out of the clear blue sky, Luna would chant to no one in particular, "Luna, Luna, Luna, would you like some tuna?" Luna loved tuna because Gram had loved tuna, and her mother and father loved tuna, too. And then she'd laugh and laugh and laugh, until her sides hurt.

"Lightning bugs!" her father echoed, as he tried very hard not to laugh.

"F-i-r-e-f-l-i-e-s! *Fireflies!*" Luna spelled out in a voice full of giggles. She wished she had brought her cheerleading megaphone with her.

"L-i-g-h-t-n-i-n-g b-u-g-s! Lightning bugs!" her father spelled back, letting go of all the laughter he had held in his belly, whooping until he shook. Luna laughed too, but this time as she pointed at her father's shoulders shaking, the stripes in his navy and white cotton shirt gently moving like a wave.

Luna and her mother and her father filled the station wagon with so much laughter that it seemed the car giggled, too. The early morning breeze of a warm summer day made its way through the open windows. It lifted the delicate hairs on Luna's caramel-toned arms and sent wisps of her hair tickling across her cheeks.

Chapter Six

Every summer, for as long as Luna could remember, she and her family drove all the way from the mountains of West Virginia to the flatlands of Missouri to visit aunts and uncles and cousins and grandparents. And with every mile, they left behind soaring mountaintops for lands as flat as pancakes.

They hung a CLOSED FOR VACATION sign on the front door of the pharmacy, directing all customers to Morrison's Pharmacy three blocks away. Luna's dad and Mr. Morrison were like brothers, having grown up together a gazillion years ago.

They always left long before the sun peeked out over the mountains, after the flickering fireflies had retreated for the night. As they passed through the capital city of Charleston, they waved goodbye to the glistening dome, and Luna tossed a gentle kiss as light as a feather in its direction.

The station wagon was packed to the gills with suitcases filled with shorts, shirts, shoes and socks. Luna's blue bicycle was hooked to the back door of the station wagon. Through the back window, she watched the colorful plastic streamers on the ends of the handlebars blowing in the hot, summer breeze.

Sometimes it was so quiet in the station wagon that her mother would say, "Luna, are you and Thistle still with us?"

"Still here, Mom," Luna replied, as Thistle ran from one side of his traveling hutch to the other. Sometimes he stood completely still; Luna thought he wanted to feel the same breeze make its way through the slender slats in his own home away from home. He would often stop running just long enough for Luna to look over and wink at him, then he'd start his daily exercise routine over, crossing his hutch again and again.

Thistle and Luna kept company in the backseat with stacks of books to read and a cooler packed with ice, bottles of water, and cartons of chocolate milk, hard-boiled eggs, a jar of bread and butter pickles, fried chicken, carrot sticks, apples, and of course, packets of tuna.

Chapter Seven

As the miles vanished, one after another, Thistle and Luna took naps. They woke just in time for lunch, as her father shut off the Plymouth's engine at a roadside park. They all sat at one of the much-loved picnic tables with the names of former visitors etched into the top, surrounded by blossoming Bradford pear trees. Luna wanted to carve her own and Henry Bloom's initials inside a heart on top of the table, but she decided to keep it to herself.

As Luna licked her fingers of the juices dripping from the bread and butter pickles, she turned the page of her English report on fireflies and showed her parents the close-up shot of a firefly's scarlet underbelly. She offered her magnifying glass from her science kit to her mom to look at the detailing, who then passed it to Luna's dad. Luna smiled at their interest and intensity. She loved it when her parents loved what she loved. Thistle even stopped munching on his lunch for a few seconds to show his support.

"*Good job,*" he seemed to say, and Luna nodded in assent.

Luna began to read from her report, which included colorful stickers of fireflies lined up across the top of each page. Miss Penny always loved a bit of artwork added to a report. It was just another reason to want to hug her close.

"Fireflies are soft-bodied beetles that are also commonly called lightning bugs."

"Ah-ha," Luna's dad exclaimed, as he put an entire half of a deviled egg in his opened mouth, followed by a most impressive gulp of chocolate milk.

"Dad, please," Luna replied, and to her surprise (then again, maybe not) Thistle covered his mouth as if to silence a chuckle.

Luna continued, "The average lifespan of fireflies is around two months. Can you imagine living for only two months?! The larval stage lasts well over a year. As it grows, the larva will repeatedly molt to shed its exoskeleton, replacing it with a larger cuticle each time. Just before updating, the firefly larva measures about three quarters of an inch in length."

As Luna finished reading, her dad held out the carrot he had just begun to eat and moving his finger along the tip, said, "About this long." Thistle began to run about his hutch with manic excitement, as if looking for his own proof of the magical, mysterious firefly, whose meaning is light—simply and beautifully, light.

Chapter Eight

As they gathered their coolers, the remaining snacks, and Thistle to return to the car, time began to tick away. The sun began to make its way down and down and down, and the moon thought about waking up and taking its place. That's when they knew they were getting closer to not only seeing those relatives who would make their hearts dance wildly, but also seeing one after another bright and shining firefly. The sun seemed to set the stage as it began to disappear, and the night began to set in.

They continued their journey west. Soon, Luna's mother and father moved their sunglasses to the tops of their head and held hands, resting them on the vinyl console. Luna loved the melding of their skin tones, light to dark, as she glanced at her own blending of the two, which always made her feel more special than anyone on earth. Every now and then, Luna's father would look through the rearview mirror and wink, or her mother would turn and wave, her brightly-colored head scarf with the design of a school of fish looking back at Luna.

And before she realized it, the words on the pages that rested in Luna's lap seemed to float off the page and get tossed up like colorful confetti, swirling all around her.

She looked to Thistle for an explanation, but he had already drifted off to sleep. Luna looked to her parents, but her mother and father were singing along with the radio to a Beatles song that Luna had heard many times before, about an idyllic world that she had decided a long time ago to believe in. After all, if you can imagine a world where a hedgehog's best friend is a pink flamingo, then anything is possible.

Luna, as if to bring a sense of normalcy back to the moment, gathered the imaginary confetti of words and rearranged them in their proper order on the seemingly blank sheet of paper in front of her and read silently. *Fireflies live in various habitats: in forests and fields and some in arid areas. They are found all over the world.*

And just as Luna drifted off to sleep, the words settled on the page.

Chapter Nine

When Luna woke, the towering Gateway to the West—the St. Louis Arch—appeared in the clear twilight distance. Thistle and Luna stretched their necks until they couldn't stretch them any farther. Thistle looked at Luna as if he wondered what was higher: the West Virginia mountains or the gleaming sight before them.

When they pulled onto the gravel driveway of Aunt Louise's and Uncle Fred's sprawling farmhouse and got out of the car, they leapt into the open arms of so many aunts, uncles, cousins, and grandparents that Luna felt giddy. Everybody hugged and kissed everybody else, and they were all suddenly aglow, just like the gathering fireflies dancing in the night: each one not fully alive without the others.

"Oh, my gosh, you're finally here!"

"And oh, how tall you've grown, Luna!"

"Do you want to go swimming?"

"Did you bring Thistle?"

"Are you hungry?"

"Hurry up, everybody! The show is about to start!"

"I'm a cheerleader now too, Luna!" Luna's cousin Jenny, who also took gymnastic classes, made this announcement through her slender megaphone. And even though everyone was talking at the same time, it all made perfect sense.

Luna and Jenny were like two peas in a pod. They were close to the same height. They were the same age. They each had a pet that they loved more than just about anything in the universe. They both loved science and math, and they were both cheerleaders. They both liked to wear cowboy boots. And, like Luna, Jenny wore a brooch in the shape of a leaf, with a tiny ladybug in the center. A framed photograph of the two of them, arms around each other, sat on Luna's desk in her room.

Instead of texting or emailing, they both liked to write and mail handwritten letters. They loved pretty stationery and colorful pens and pencils. Each time they mailed an envelope, they chose a stamp depicting an animal, a flower, an important person—or even a Popsicle: that one could be scratched and sniffed. On the envelope's flap, they lined up stickers or melted red candle wax at the center, pressing down with a brass stamp in the design of a butterfly.

All of a sudden, the farm dogs ran up to them and jumped higher and higher to plant kisses on all of their faces. Not a single one of the family was bothered by their continual licking. They all just smiled and took turns stroking their fur.

Even though Luna wanted to do everything her cousins wanted to do, the night sky was turning velvety dark, with too many stars to count. The show was about to begin, and Jenny grabbed Luna's hand. All the cousins ran towards the summer house to get ready. Luna knew that the glass jars would be lined up on a shelf inside, the screw-on lids poked with holes as they each caught first one firefly then another, knowing all the time that they'd set them free to keep on dancing in the night, knowing that they'd gather every night—every single night. And knowing that—all of that—made them all very happy, made them all feel part of something bigger and more beautiful than any of them could imagine.

"Look, over there. Do you see them?" Jenny asked.

As Luna grabbed her glass jar, she answered, "I do! I see them! Their underbellies are spectacular, no matter how many times I see them."

"I know! What color do you like best, yellow

or green?"

"I don't know, but if I had to choose, I'd say yellow, because it reminds me of butterscotch!"

"Oh, that's so cool! I love butterscotch!"

"How about you?"

"If I had to choose, I'd say green, because it reminds me of Rio!"

"Definitely! I love Rio so much!"

Rio was Jenny's pet parakeet. He didn't say much, but what he did say was almost always awesome.

"I'm trying to teach him to say fireflies, but so far all he's managed to say is fly. We're working on it."

"Yep, that's what we do. We work on it." Luna and Jenny breathed in the crispness of the night air, the dew resting light as a feather on their summer-warm skin as they continued their merry jaunt through the night.

Chapter Ten

As Luna, Jenny, and all the other cousins plopped down to rest on soft, weathered cushions scattered throughout the summer house, Jenny's older brother Josh descended the rickety attic ladder and dropped a big, worn cardboard box labeled **FIREFLIES** with a thud. Suddenly, everybody scrambled to reach it first, knowing what treasures awaited.

Thistle and Rio looked on, as if they too were a very important part of the gathering of relatives and beckoning fireflies. Rio flitted from one side of his birdcage to the other, and

Thistle mimicked his travels. Every now and then the two would stop as if on cue, look at each other and everyone, then resume their spirited journeys.

The girls placed jeweled tiaras on top of their heads and twirled about like fairy princesses, while the boys tied on red capes to join in the dance of the fireflies. They ran through the yard, following the twinkling lights as they blinked here, there, and everywhere, each one following their tiny lead with more joy than they thought possible.

The fireflies were like a gathering of fairies, each neon yellow, green, or orange light glowing in its own unique brightness. Their random flashing and twinkling seemed like stars falling from the sky, their bellies sparkling like glitter. As Luna and Jenny and all the others held a firefly loosely in their clasped palms, the light seemed to make them glow, too. And even in their smallness, they felt magical.

Soon there would be more fireflies dancing in the night than Luna could count. And she stood still for more than a few minutes, trying with all her power to figure out a way to capture the wonderment of the moment, put it in a jar, and seal it tight so that she could open it and recapture it all, long after the fireflies had fallen asleep.

As the late darkness of each long summer night grew, more and more fireflies gathered and leapt and shone, until it seemed to Luna that a well-rehearsed ballet was lighting up the night sky, the prima ballerina sending out invitations to all fireflies to join her. No one could resist her call; parents, aunts and uncles, and everyone who had gathered looked all around, marveling at the fireflies dancing in the midnight sky.

Luna closed her eyes and used all her senses to remember as much of the evenings as she could, long after they had left their Missouri relatives, filing each one away to revisit whenever she wanted to re-experience the magic. She stored each sound, each image, each ounce of the night sky's crisp air on her

skin, and tasted every s'more that was held over an open fire. She knew she would revisit each one over and over in her mind, until she could return.

Chapter Eleven

When the time to leave came much too soon, Luna and her family made their way back through Kentucky to West Virginia, waving to galloping horses on lush, green meadows. Once again, Luna closed her eyes, imagining all the fireflies dancing in the night and the horses trying to keep up with the flashes of golden yellow light.

As they made their way east, Thistle sat on a soft, gray, cotton blanket next to Luna, who stroked his quills, soothing Thistle until his eyes began to close. Luna pulled her English paper on fireflies from her backpack and read the closing paragraphs.

Firefly light is intermittent. Each blinking pattern is a signal that helps them find their potential partners. There are more than 2,000 species worldwide. They are very diverse. The flashes of light are usually from males looking for females. It is a twinkling conversation. Some fireflies blink in unison.

Fireflies are not only magical and mysterious, they also seem to join one another in a chorus of light that, when set to music, gifts observers with a most melodious symphony of light and color and energy and possibility. They might each begin the chorus separately, but in the end, they come together to reach a crescendo that is, like all pure beauty, indescribable.

When Luna and Thistle and their family made their way back to the mountains, the night had slipped in. Luna slid underneath her familiar flower garden quilt as the night coolness made its way through the screens of her open bedroom windows. She blew Jenny a kiss, then thought about Henry Bloom and what a new school year might bring. Luna glanced outside her window to see the flicker of fireflies dancing in the night, each flash meeting with the chorus of cicadas. The family all fell asleep to the sounds and lights of another long summer day's closing, knowing that they would end—hoping they wouldn't.

"*The lightning bug is brilliant
but he hasn't any mind
he blunders through existence
with his headlight on behind.*"

—Anonymous, late 1800s

Acknowledgments

I am deeply grateful to the following passionate readers who read my work over and over, in every stage, from beginning to end. I could not (nor would I even attempt to) do what I do without them. Their guidance and wisdom, vision and patience are immeasurable: Ella Morgan Dillon for her gentle, but very certain nudging in convincing me to step outside my comfort zone; Katy Smith, friend and voracious reader, for reminding me of the prima ballerina's ballet in the sky; Olivia Matras, a very special, young reader of a very early draft of the story and her mother, Katie Matras, for making time, every single time; and Laura Miller, whose support and passion for a good story made its way to West Virginia from Kansas. She's a bit like Dorothy. Together, they have enough gold stars to light up the night sky, except for the brightest one, which will always be reserved for my husband, John, who believes that every word I write is magical.

Enormous thanks to my incredibly talented illustrator, Carly Thaw, whose vision brought my words to life in a way that far exceeded even my lofty expectations.

Tremendous gratitude to my publisher, Janie Jessee, and the entire team at Jan-Carol Publishing, Inc., especially the erudite editors. I am not worthy.

Thank you, too, to booksellers, librarians, and readers from around the country who choose to read my work and pass it along to other voracious readers. Your generous spirit is so very treasured.

I would also like to thank Brad Paisley, fellow West Virginian, for his spirited song, "Southern Comfort Zone," which I listened to over and over and over again, as I drove to my writing studio in Fayetteville, WV, from my home in Charleston, encouraging me to stay true to what I knew to be true.

Finally, I'd like to remember and thank my great-aunt, Dora Roling, for telling me stories late at night, under a mound of calico quilts that carried the scent of lavender, when my age was in single digits. I remember each and every one. I didn't know then that they would serve me so well, as I penned stories of my own. I didn't know then the true measure of their worth. I didn't know then that one story in particular would be the seed of my first story for young readers, a planting that has gifted so very much.

Kathleen M. Jacobs

is the author of the critically-
acclaimed YA-novel, *Honeysuckle
Holiday* and *Betsy Blossom Brown*.
Sophie & the Bookmobile was the author's first
early chapter book. Her other works include
Marble Town, a book for the MG-reader. Her
first children's book, *Please Close It!* has enjoyed
numerous awards, and her chapbooks *The
Puppeteer of Objects: A Lyrical Poem* and *Collected
Curiosities: Poems, Essays & Opinions* offer insights
into human behavior and understanding. She is
a former teacher of English and Creative Writing,
and holds a M.A. in Humanistic Studies. She was
the 2017 New River Gorge Writer-in-Residence.
In 2020, she was chosen Runner-up Best Author
of WV by *WV Living*.

www.kathleenmjacobs.com
@kathleenm.jacobs

CPSIA information can be obtained
at www.ICGtesting.com
Printed in the USA
LVHW021643310321
683084LV00011B/1573

9 781950 895915